Can You

Hawkeye Collins & Amy Adams in
The Case of the
Mysterious
Dognapper
& 9 Other Mysteries

Created by Bruce Lansky

Meadowbrook Press
Distributed by Simon & Schuster
New York

Library of Congress Cataloging-In-Publication Data

This title was previously cataloged with the following information: Masters, M.
Hawkeye Collins & Amy Adams in the case of the mysterious dognapper and other mysteries.
At head of title: Can you solve the mystery?
Summary: Two twelve-year-old sleuths, solve ten puzzling cases, using sketches of important
clues. Includes hints for interpreting clues and brief explanations of investigative methods used.
[1. Mystery and detective stories. 2. Literary recreations.] I. Title. II. Title: Case
of the mysterious dognapper and other mysteries.
PZ7.M42392Hb   1983   [Fic] 83-873

ISBN: 978-1-4424-6902-0

Editor: Kathe Grooms
Assistant Editor: Louise Delagran, Alicia Ester
Cover Design: Tamara JM Peterson
Design: Stephen Cardot, Terry Dugan
Production: John Ware, Donna Ahrens, Pamela Barnard, Daryl Peterson
Illustrations: Stephen Cardot
Interior Hand Photography: Tamara JM Peterson
Hand Model: Emily Peterson
All stories written by Alexander von Wacker, with the exception of:
"The Mystery of the Moody Medallion" and "The Case of the Stashed Cash"
      written by Nancy Crochiere
"The Mystery of the Double-Crossed Inheritance," written by Rosalyn Stendahl

20 19 18 17 16 15 14   15 14 13 12 11 10 9 8 7 6 5 4 3

Printed in USA

Contents

Amy Adams   Hawkeye Collins

Young Sleuths Detect Fun in Mysteries

By Alice Cory
Staff Writer

Lakewood Hills has two new super sleuths watching over its citizens. They are Christoper "Hawkeye" Collins and Amy Amanda Adams, both 12 years old and sixth-grade students at Lakewood Hills Elementary.

Christopher Collins, the popular, blond, blue-eyed sleuth

of 128 Crestview Drive, is better known by his nickname, "Hawkeye." His father, Peter Collins, who is an attorney downtown, explains, "We started calling him Hawkeye many years ago because he notices everything, even tiny details. That's what makes him so good at solving mysteries." His mother, Linda Collins, a real estate agent, agrees: "Yes, but he

Sleuths continues on page 4A

Sleuths continued from 1A

also started to draw at a very early age. His sketches capture everything he sees. He draws clues or the scene of the crime — or anything else that will help solve a mystery."

Amy Adams, a spitfire with red hair and sparkling green eyes, lives right across the street, at 131 Crestview Drive. Known to many as the star of the track team, she is also a star math student. "She's quick of mind, quick of foot and quick of temper," says her teacher, Ted Bronson, chuckling. "And she's never intimidated." Not only do she and Hawkeye share the same birthday, but also the same love of mysteries.

"If something's wrong," says Amy, leaning on her bike, "you just can't look the other way."

"Right," says Hawkeye, pulling his ever-present sketch pad and pencil from his back pocket. "And if we can't solve a case right away, I'll do a drawing of the scene of the crime. When we study my sketch, we can usually figure out what happened."

When the two detectives are not playing video games or soccer (Hawkeye is the captain of the sixth-grade team), they can often be seen biking around town, making sure justice is done. Occa-

sionally aided by Hawkeye's frisky golden retriever, Nosey, and Amy's six-year-old sister, Lucy, they've solved every case they've handled to date.

How did the two get started in the detective business?

It all started last year at Lakewood Hills Elementary's Career Days. There the two met Sergeant Treadwell, one of Lakewood Hills' best-known policemen. Of Hawkeye and Amy, Sergeant Treadwell proudly brags, "They're terrific. Right after we met, one of the teachers had a whole pile of tests stolen. I sure couldn't figure out who had done it, but Hawkeye did one of his sketches and he and Amy had the case solved in five minutes! You can't fool those two."

Sergeant Treadwell adds: "I don't know what Lakewood Hills ever did without Hawkeye and Amy. They've found a dognapped dog, located stolen video games, and cracked many other tough cases. Why, whenever I have a problem I can't solve, I know just where to go — straight to those two super sleuths!"

> " They've found a dognapped dog, located stolen video games, and cracked many other tough cases. "

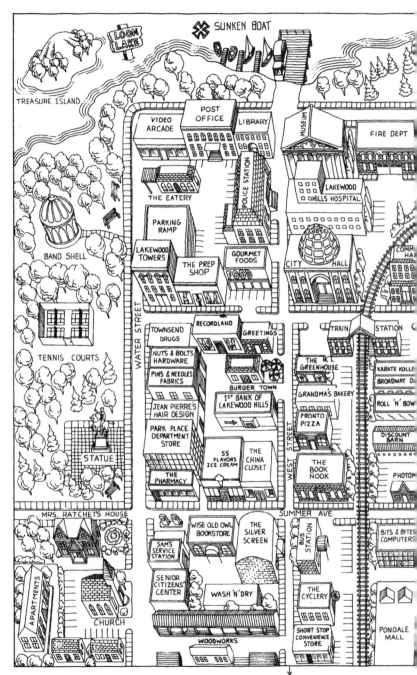

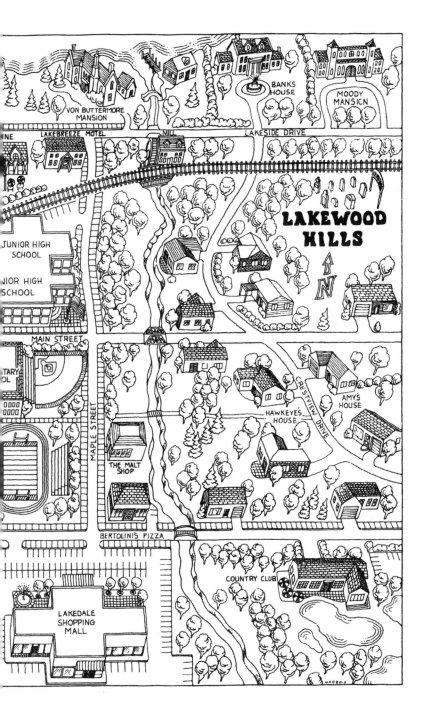

Dear Readers,

You can solve these mysteries along with us! Start by reading very carefully — — Watch out for things like what people <u>say</u> happened, the ways they behave, and details like the time and the weather.

Then look closely at the sketch or other picture clue with the story. If you remember the facts, the picture clue should help you break the case.

<u>I</u>f you want to check your answer — — or if a hard case stumps you — — turn to the solutions at the back of the book. They're written in mirror type. Hold them up to a mirror and they'll look right. If you don't have a mirror, turn the page and hold it up to the light. (You can teach yourself to read backwards, too. We can do it pretty well now and it comes in handy some-times in our cases.)

Have fun — — we sure did!

Hawkeye   *Amy*

The Case of the Imperfect Crime

Hawkeye spotted the jade earring lying in the shag carpet of the family room.

"Found it, Mom!" he shouted.

Hawkeye snatched up the earring and went into the kitchen. There he found his mother poking through the drawers. His father, on his knees, was searching beneath the breakfast table. Nosey, Hawkeye's frisky golden retriever, had her head in the garbage.

"At last," said Mr. Collins with a sigh of relief.

"Good going, Hawkeye." Mrs. Collins took the earring from Hawkeye and patted her son on the back. "I knew if anyone could find it, you could."

"Well, Mom, you just have to figure out where it could be and then use your eyes," Hawkeye said.

"Yes, but you've got a pair of great eyes—that makes all the difference. We're just ordinary human beings," Mr. Collins said, chuckling.

Mrs. Collins, glad that the search for the earring was over, shut the cupboards and drawers.

"On Tuesday night, I looked for over an hour for my car keys," said Mr. Collins. Proudly, he added, "When Hawkeye came home from the computer camp meeting, he found them within five minutes."

"Well, you've earned your nickname this week, Hawkeye—even if you haven't had any mysteries to solve yet." Mrs. Collins smiled at her son.

Just then, someone knocked frantically at the Collins' front door. Nosey, scrambling and barking, tipped over the garbage as she bounded off to the door.

"I'll see who it is!" said Hawkeye, running after his dog.

"What about the garbage?" said Mr. Collins. "Oh, never mind, I'll get it."

Hawkeye and Nosey hurried to the front of the house. Hawkeye clutched Nosey's collar and swung open the front door. Mrs. Peterson, their grey-haired neighbor, had her fist in the air, ready to knock again.

"Hawkeye, my phone line's been cut!" She burst past Hawkeye and Nosey into the house. "Quick, call the police. I've been robbed!" She twisted her hands together. "Oh, how terrible. Hawkeye, are your parents home?"

"Sure, I'll get 'em." He raced to the back of the house. "Mom, Dad! Call Sergeant Treadwell! Mrs. Peterson's been robbed!"

Ever since meeting Sergeant Treadwell last year, Hawkeye had worked with him on a number of cases. While Mrs. Collins phoned the police station, Hawkeye and his father returned to the front hall.

"Oh, Mr. Collins, it's so awful," said Mrs. Peterson. "I went to the store, and when I came back, I sensed right away that something was wrong. I went to the living room and the sliding glass door to the patio was wide open. Broken glass was everywhere. Someone broke in and stole the painting my grandfather left me!"

"Were they gone when you got back?" asked Hawkeye. "Did they take anything else?"

"Oh, yes, they were gone." Mrs. Peterson thought for a moment. "And, yes, I think they took some other things as well. I'm not quite sure what, though. I just saw the empty space on the wall, screamed, and ran to the phone. But the cord had been cut!"

"Terrible," said Mr. Collins, shaking his head. "There have been so many thefts of paintings lately. What does Sergeant Treadwell call the thief? Whistler's Brother. I wonder if it could be him again."

"That's possible," said Mrs. Peterson. "I heard about two paintings being stolen that way just last week. It might be the same robber."

Mr. Collins, who was a lawyer, said, "I handled your grandfather's will and I remember that painting." He shook his head sadly. "It was quite valuable. I hope you had it insured."

"It was worth $50,000!" Mrs. Peterson covered her eyes and shook her head. "And I'm not sure if it was on my insurance policy or not."

Hawkeye whistled. "Wow, $50,000. That's all the money I'd need for the rest of my life. But don't worry. Mom called Sergeant Treadwell and he should be here any second. Maybe Amy and I can help, too. You know Amy, Mrs. Peterson—she lives across the street. She's not home now, but she'll be back from track practice in about an hour. "

Mrs. Peterson sighed. "Thank you, Hawkeye. I've heard how good you two are at this type of thing."

"Is there anyone besides Whistler's Brother who might have stolen the painting?" asked Hawkeye. "Can you think of any other suspects?"

Mrs. Peterson thought for a moment. "Well, I did have to fire a cleaning lady just two weeks ago. I caught her stealing some change from my dresser."

Sergeant Treadwell, rather pudgy and a little bald, arrived a few minutes later. The sergeant, Hawkeye, and Mr. Collins all went over to Mrs. Peterson's house. It was a warm night and fairly quiet in the neighborhood. Mrs. Peterson's ranch-style house was similar to Hawkeye's.

"Hawkeye," said Sergeant Treadwell as he led the way into the house, "I didn't bring a camera, so maybe you could do a drawing of the scene of the crime for me." It was well known in Lakewood Hills that Hawkeye had won statewide contests for his sketches and that he often solved mysteries by sketching the scenes of crimes.

"You bet, Sarge."

"And do it like you always do—nice and realistic, with all the details."

Hawkeye had his sketch pad and pencil with him, as usual, in his back pocket. "Sure. You know, Mrs. Peterson thinks that either the guy you call Whistler's Brother or her old cleaning lady stole the painting."

"Could be, could be. Oops!" Sergeant Treadwell tripped on the edge of a rug and stumbled to the floor. "Ah," he said in a professional tone of voice, trying to cover up his clumsiness, "maybe there are a few clues down here."

Mr. Collins winked at Hawkeye and went out the open patio door. "I'll look around out here. Maybe I'll find something."

Hawkeye stood silently in a corner of the living room. He carefully studied the room and noted a few things that seemed out of place. Squinting out of one eye, then the other, he paced back and forth, then started his sketch.

Hawkeye drew the room quickly, beginning with the walls, the door, and the rug. He filled in the couch and the tables, and, finally, put in all the clues he had spotted with his keen eyes.

Hawkeye thought to himself, "That's strange—whoever took the painting ignored the set of silverware, the wallet full of cash, and the other painting!"

As he put the finishing touches on the drawing, he realized something else—something shocking.

"Wow!" he said out loud. "Hey, Sarge, look at this. I know who stole Mrs. Peterson's painting!"

WHO STOLE MRS. PETERSON'S PAINTING?

Find the solution on page 79

"Someone broke in and stole the painting my grandfather left me!"
said Mrs. Peterson.

The Case of the
Mysterious
Dognapper

Hawkeye and Amy rode their bikes up the steep driveway to the von Buttermore mansion. With its twin towers and slate roof, the stone house looked like an enormous castle.

"This house looks bigger every time we come here," said Hawkeye.

"Sure does." Amy stood up and pedaled her bike with all her strength. "Do you think Mrs. von Buttermore ever gets lost in it?"

"No, she was born here. She'd know it by now."

Both of them were more dressed up than they had been in a long time. Hawkeye's blonde hair was neatly combed and he wore his favorite collared shirt and a brand-new pair of jeans. He even had a new sketch pad in his back pocket, and his glasses were spotless. Amy, his friend and fellow sleuth from across the street, was wearing a new, pink button-down shirt and clean jeans.

The two sleuths wanted to look their best because they were going to ask Mrs. von Buttermore to help pay for the new youth center.

"Whatever she says," said Amy, "it sure is nice of her to let us talk to her on the Fourth of July."

Mrs. von Buttermore was the richest person in Lakewood Hills. She loved to donate things, particularly to kids. She personally had chosen and paid for all of the fireworks for that evening's Fourth of July celebration.

"Now, remember," said Hawkeye, "we have to thank her for the fireworks first. Then we start talking about the youth center."

"Do you really think she'll help pay for one?" asked Amy.

Hawkeye shrugged. "She said she wanted to when she talked to Dad this morning. But she wanted to talk to us first to see exactly how kids might use it."

They parked their bikes at a fountain in front of the mansion. A terribly proper butler in a tuxedo greeted them at the door.

"Welcome," said the butler. He stared into the air above their heads. "Mrs. von Buttermore is waiting in the drawing room," he added, in a strong English accent.

"Wow, I didn't know she had a whole room just for drawing," Hawkeye whispered as they followed the butler.

Amy whispered back, "No, silly. That's just another word for living room."

They followed the butler down one hall and through another. Every wall and corner was filled with paintings and antiques. In one corner was a life-size statue of a horse; in another was a shiny set of medieval armor.

The butler swung open a large pair of doors. Mrs. von Buttermore sat next to a sunny window, a large sketch pad and a drawing pen in hand. Priceless, her enormous black and white Great Dane, lay at her feet.

"Good morning, Hawkeye and Amy!" she said with a big smile. She set her pad and pen aside. "I just love to draw—but I'm afraid I'm just not as good as you, Hawkeye."

Hawkeye winked at Amy. "Hi, Mrs. von Buttermore," he said, turning to face her.

"How are you?" asked Amy.

"Wonderful, wonderful."

Amy looked at the dog. "You know, every time I come here I'm always surprised at how big Priceless is."

Hawkeye nodded. "Yeah, he's twice as big as Nosey!"

Mrs. von Buttermore smiled proudly and turned to her butler. "Ives, I wonder if you would mind taking Priceless out for a little air while I chat with Hawkeye and Amy."

The butler nodded curtly. "Ah-choo!" he sneezed. "Pardon me. Certainly, Madam." He turned and started out of the room. "Come along, Priceless. Be a good dog and don't dawdle. Ahhh-choo! Ahhh-chooo!"

The dog stood and stretched, then trotted like a pony out of the room. After they had left, Amy was the first to speak.

"Oh, thank you so much for the fireworks, Mrs. von Buttermore," said Amy as fast as she could. "I'm sure all the kids are going to love them."

"You're welcome, Amy," said Mrs. von Buttermore. "Now, why don't you two tell me about the youth center? What kinds of things should it have? If you are going to be the ones to use it, I think you should take part in its development."

"Well," began Amy, "everyone likes to roller skate in the summer and ice skate in the winter."

"And a lot of kids like basketball, too," said Hawkeye. "And maybe there should be a place for movies and..."

Just then Ives, the butler, burst into the room. His tuxedo, which had been spotless when he left with Priceless, was now torn and dirty.

"Oh, Madam, something simply awful has just occurred," he blurted out, then struggled to look dignified.

"Ives, what is it?" gasped Mrs. von Buttermore.

"As I walked Priceless past his doghouse, two men attacked us! I tried to resist them, Madam—I even tried to fight back, as best I could. But they hit me over the head. When I regained my senses, Priceless was gone."

Mrs. von Buttermore clutched at her heart. "Priceless? You mean they kidnapped Priceless?"

Ives nodded. "It appears so, Madam."

She fell back into her chair. "Oh, my baby, my poor baby."

Amy hurried over to a gold telephone. "I'll call Sergeant Treadwell right away."

Hawkeye looked at Mrs. von Buttermore, whose eyes were brimming with tears. He scratched his head, trying to think of the right thing to say.

"Don't worry, Mrs. von Buttermore, we'll get Priceless back. Amy and I always solve the case." Hawkeye turned to Ives. "Did you get a good look at the men? Did you notice anything about them?"

Ives looked at Hawkeye for the first time that day. "Well, actually, I didn't," he said.

Hawkeye took out his pad and pencil. "Don't you remember anything?"

"Well, the two men were rather large and monstrous."

"Did they have a car?" asked Hawkeye impatiently.

Ives thought. "I'm afraid I can't say," he said at last. "They knocked me out, you know."

"Oh, dear," sighed Mrs. von Buttermore. "It seems as though we don't have any clues at all."

"Well," said Amy, "I called Sergeant Treadwell. He'll be here right away."

"Thank you, dear," said Mrs. von Buttermore as she wiped her eyes with her silk handkerchief. "Ives, that will be all for now. Why don't you go and tidy up."

Ives straightened his torn shirt. "Yes, Madam. I shall do so at once." Shreds of torn cloth flapped as he left.

"Oh, Hawkeye and Amy, what am I going to do?" cried Mrs. von Buttermore. "Priceless means the world to me."

"Once Sarge gets here," said Amy, "we'll go out and take a look at the scene of the crime. Hey, does anyone have a motive? I mean, if you knew someone who had a reason to hurt you or Priceless, that might be a lead."

"Yeah," said Hawkeye. "Do you know anyone who doesn't like Priceless?"

"Someone who doesn't like Priceless?" gasped Mrs. von Buttermore. "Impossible!"

Amy tried again. "Well, did anyone ever complain about Priceless? Or did Priceless ever attack anyone?"

Mrs. von Buttermore hesitated. "Well, Priceless was rather fond of the milkman and the gardener."

"Fond?" asked Hawkeye, confused.

"Yes. Fond. Fond of their taste," said Mrs. von Buttermore. "He's tasted the gardener three or four times, and the milkman twice."

Hawkeye's mouth dropped open. "You mean he bit them?" he asked.

"Please, Hawkeye, you needn't put it so harshly."

There was a gentle knock on the drawing room doors.

"Come in," called Mrs. von Buttermore.

Ives stepped in. He had cleaned up and changed into another tuxedo.

"Madam, the day's mail has just arrived."

"Oh, really, Ives, later. I simply couldn't think about anything except Priceless right now."

Ives coughed. "Yes, but Madam, I think there's something here you ought to see."

He stepped forward, silver tray in hand. On the tray lay an envelope.

"Oh, wow!" cried Amy, noticing the envelope.

It was a plain white envelope. On it, in large letters between the address and the stamp, was the message, "DO YOU WANT YOUR DOG BACK?"

Mrs. von Buttermore cried, "Oh, give it to me!" and snatched the letter from the tray.

Hands shaking, she tore open the enve-lope. Inside she found a sheet of paper with a typewritten message. She read the letter and then, starting to cry again, dropped it.

"Oh, poor Priceless! I must get him back! Quickly, Ives, call for my limousine. I must go to the bank at once!"

Hawkeye picked up the ransom note. Together he and Amy read through it.

A moment later, the two sleuths raised their heads, almost in unison.

"Wait, Mrs. von Buttermore!" Hawkeye shouted. "Sergeant Treadwell will be here in a minute, and he'll be able to nab your dognapper without you having to pay a cent!"

"Hawkeye, what on earth are you talking about?" asked Mrs. von Buttermore.

"He means," said Amy, a smile spreading across her face, "that we know who the dognapper is."

WHO WAS THE DOGNAPPER AND HOW DID HAWKEYE AND AMY KNOW WHO IT WAS?

Find the solution on page 81

July 3

Dear Mrs. von Buttermore:
When you get this, your black dog will be in a cage in the centre of an empty room. He'll stay there forever if you don't give us $20,000 cash. If you ever want to see Priceless again, you'd better do as we say. We'll ring up later with instructions.

Yours truly,
The Dognappers

Ives coughed. "Yes, but Madam,
I think there's something here you ought to see."

The Mystery of the
Moody
Medallion

"I can't believe no one has been living here for six months now," Amy said to Hawkeye. They stood with Nosey on the sagging front porch of the old Moody mansion.

"Yeah, ever since Mr. Moody died."

In his will, Mr. Moody had left the old house to his nephew in California. But the nephew couldn't return to Lakewood Hills immediately. As Mr. Moody's lawyer, Hawkeye's father had been checking on the house twice a week. Because he was very busy this week, Mr. Collins had asked Hawkeye to check the Moody mansion for him.

"Do you really think it's haunted?" Amy asked.

"I don't know," Hawkeye replied. "But it's plenty creepy. The only good thing about this job is that Dad said I could look for the old medallion Mr. Moody left me."

The old man had taken a liking to Hawkeye and, knowing that Hawkeye liked puzzles, had left a riddle for him in his will.

"If I can solve the riddle, I can have the medallion," said Hawkeye. "It's gold!"

Hawkeye unlocked the front door and swung it open. He and Amy stared into the dark, silent house, then took several cautious steps in, followed by Nosey. Suddenly, a strong draft of air slammed the front door shut behind them.

"Oh, my heart," said Amy, dramatically. "That scared me to death!"

"Really." Hawkeye patted Nosey, who was huddled up against him.

Brushing aside cobwebs and tiptoeing on the creaking wood floor, they made their way through one dark room after another. Finally they came to a large room, the walls of which were covered with old portraits.

"This is it!" Hawkeye whispered excitedly. "Mr. Moody's study!"

Trying not to shiver, Amy said, "But why here? Why not in another room?"

"Take a look at this." Hawkeye pulled a crumpled piece of paper from his pocket and handed it to Amy. "Read the riddle."

Aloud, she read:

"'The eyes of friends guard my medallion,
But one face alone will aid you, sleuth.
If you look where I lead, you never will find it,
But behind my back, you may find the truth.'"

Amy scratched her head. "What's it mean?"

"Well," said Hawkeye as he paced around the room, "Mr. Moody was an artist and he painted all these pictures himself."

"Oh, I get it." Amy went up to one of the paintings. "If these guys are his friends, and the eyes of his friends are guarding his medallion, then the medallion should be hidden somewhere in this room."

"Yep," agreed Hawkeye. "So let's start searching."

They divided the room in half and examined every crack in the walls and every loose board on the floor. They rummaged through an old desk and a musty trunk, and checked for loose bricks in the fireplace. But they had no luck.

"These places are too obvious," Amy said finally. She chewed thoughtfully on a fingernail. "Hey, I've got an idea. 'Behind my back' might mean behind a picture."

"Good idea, Amy. Let's check it out."

Hawkeye and Amy searched behind each portrait, but with no more success than before. Discouraged, they sat on the dusty desk and wondered what to do next.

"Maybe the medallion isn't in this room, after all," Amy sighed.

Hawkeye did not respond. He was staring at one of the portraits: a painting of a man with a full head of wild, uncombed brown hair.

"Amy," he said suddenly, "look at that painting. That's Mr. Moody as a young man. I didn't even recognize him."

"Hey, a self-portrait. Cool," said Amy. "And if the riddle says that the truth is behind his back, then the medallion must be hidden somewhere behind *that* painting."

They raced over and searched every inch of the portrait and the wall behind it, but again found nothing.

"I don't understand," said Amy. "Maybe he didn't leave the medallion. Maybe..."

Just then, they heard a noise on the stairs. As it came closer, they froze. Hawkeye was about to yell, "Run for it, Amy!" when a black nose sniffed under the door.

"Nosey!" called Hawkeye.

Amy let out a sigh of relief and Hawkeye rolled his eyes.

"Whew," he said. "That kind of scared me."

"Kind of," Amy commented sarcastically. "Hey, do a sketch, Hawkeye. That always helps."

"Good idea." He pulled his sketch pad and pencil from his back pocket.

Hawkeye carefully studied Mr. Moody's self-portrait, and then began to draw both the picture and the wall it hung on. He made sure he drew in all the boards and nails and every other detail he could see.

When he was finished, he and Amy sat down on a sheet-covered couch and studied the drawing. They thought long and hard, but neither sleuth could solve the riddle. Finally, Hawkeye heaved a sigh and leaned back against the sofa, cupping his head in his hands.

"This is a real tough case—and Mr. Moody isn't around to give us another clue," said Amy, glumly.

"Maybe if we look at the riddle again, it'll help," suggested Hawkeye, pulling it out of his pocket.

Amy read through it and glanced back at Hawkeye's drawing. Suddenly, her green eyes brightened.

"Got it! There's more behind Mr. Moody's back than just a wall," she said. "Hawkeye, I think I know where the medallion is!"

WHERE WAS THE MEDALLION HIDDEN?

Find the solution on page 83

"Got it! There's more behind Mr. Moody's back than just a wall," Amy said.

The Case of the
Stashed
Cash

As Hawkeye and Amy made their way down the street toward the video arcade, Mr. Bertolini, the owner of the best pizza shop in Lakewood Hills, came rushing after them.

"Hawkeye, Amy!" he shouted, dashing up to them. "You have to help me!"

"Hey, take your time," said Amy.

"Yeah, catch your breath." Hawkeye motioned toward the arcade. "We've got plenty of time. We were just going to play some video games."

Mr. Bertolini swallowed and started again. "You know Frank, my night manager? Well, last night

I caught him with his hand in the cash register. It turns out he's been stealing from me for years."

Hawkeye's eyes widened in surprise. "Wow, what a bummer."

"Really," said Amy. "Have you gone to the police yet?"

"Oh, sure," said Mr. Bertolini, wringing his hands in his apron. "Frank told them he'd hidden three thousand dollars—but he won't say where. Sergeant Treadwell got a warrant and searched his apartment. But he didn't find the money, and he's convinced that it isn't there."

"Didn't he find anything at all?" asked Amy. "Any clues or anything?"

Mr. Bertolini threw his hands up. "The only thing he found was a note Frank had written to his girlfriend."

He pulled a copy of the note from his apron pocket and read it aloud. "'Mary, dear, I've hidden the money right under their noses. In case they get me—Mr. Bertolini was looking at me kind of funny the other day—here are directions to the cash: Knight to K2.'"

When he heard the message, Hawkeye remembered something. "Hey, you don't suppose that's the same Mary who worked for you a year ago?"

"Oh, yes, Mary Knight." Mr. Bertolini smiled. "I bet it is."

"Well, that solves one part of the mystery," said Amy. "And I bet 'right under their noses' means in the pizza shop."

"But what could 'K2' mean?" asked Hawkeye. "Let's go back to the pizza shop and take a look around."

Mr. Bertolini led the way. "Be my guests."

The three of them hurried back to the shop and started to search it. While Amy and Mr. Bertolini looked all over the kitchen—even in the freezer— Hawkeye sat down in the dining room and started to sketch.

Suddenly, the wall behind the counter caught Hawkeye's attention.

"Hey!" he said, calling them into the room, "maybe the 'K' stands for your king-size pizza."

"Yeah!" said Amy. A moment later, though, her smile faded. "But that doesn't make any sense. Frank couldn't have hidden the money in a pizza—at least, not without someone getting a mouthful of hundred-dollar bills."

Hawkeye continued with his drawing. "I guess you're right." With a weak smile, he added, "Besides, it would have been too obvious to hide the money in the dough."

Amy slapped her forehead and groaned. "Oh, brother."

She and Mr. Bertolini started to search the restaurant. Hawkeye continued his drawing.

A few minutes later, Amy came by and peered over Hawkeye's shoulder. "Nice job of sketching, Hawkeye—hey, wait a second." She thought hard for a moment, then brightened.

"I know where Frank hid the dough—I mean, the money!"

WHERE HAD FRANK HIDDEN THE MONEY?

Find the solution on page 85

"Hey!" Hawkeye said, "Maybe the 'K' stands for your king-size pizza."

The Mystery of the
Double-
Crossed
Inheritance

Hawkeye's parents hadn't been gone more than a minute when he and Amy got out a flashlight and began to sneak toward Mr. Collins' study.

Just outside the study, Hawkeye stopped and listened intently for the sound of the car. When he was sure it was safe, he led the way in.

"We've got to be quick about finding the will and reading it," said Hawkeye, switching on the flashlight. "Mom and Dad just went to the corner store, and if Dad catches me in his study, I'll be grounded for a week."

"No sweat." Amy hurried over to a window, lifted the curtain, and looked out into the dark night. "All's clear so far."

Turning back to Hawkeye, she shook her head. "There's just got to be something wrong with Mr. Mendez's will."

As the lawyer representing Mr. Mendez's estate, Mr. Collins had read the will to Mr. Mendez's relatives the night before. To everyone's surprise, Mr. Mendez hadn't left most of his money to his favorite niece, Christina, and her girls' school. Instead, he had left almost all the money to his other niece, an Englishwoman named Miss Pleasance.

"Miss Pleasance wasn't even around when Mr. Mendez was sick," said Hawkeye. "I mean, she's lived in England forever doing that—what do you call it?—that calligraphy stuff for a greeting card company."

"Really. Christina always helped Mr. Mendez. And he loved her school, too. I heard he left her a few things and a little money, but..." Amy thought of Mr. Mendez and smiled. "He sure was a nice old man. It was real nice of him to leave me that rolltop desk."

"Yeah, and to leave me that autographed copy of *The Hound of the Baskervilles*," said Hawkeye. "I've really got a rare-book collection now."

His voice dropping to a whisper, Hawkeye said, "We've got to be quick. I think the will's in Dad's briefcase. And don't turn on the light. If you do, my folks will see it when they drive in."

By the beam of the flashlight, they made their way over to Mr. Collins' desk. They found the briefcase, set it on the desk, and undid the latches.

"Oh, boy," said Hawkeye, glancing at Amy. "I sure feel like a criminal. I hope Dad doesn't find out about this."

"Just speed it up and he won't."

Hawkeye aimed the flashlight at the will. They quickly read through it once, but didn't find anything remarkable. They read it a second time.

Disappointed, Amy shook her head. "I sure don't see anything strange here, Hawkeye."

"I don't either, but there's just *got* to be something wrong with the will." He pushed his glasses back up on his nose. "Why would Mr. Mendez leave so much money to that Miss Pleasance? It doesn't make any sense."

They read through the will one more time. Suddenly, Hawkeye gasped.

"Hey, Amy, look at this!"

But before Hawkeye could explain, the overhead light flashed on. Mr. Collins stood in the doorway.

WHAT DID HAWKEYE AND AMY FIND IN THE WILL?

Find the solution on page 87

Last Will and Testament

I, Joseph Manuel Mendez, being of sound mind and body, do on this tenth day of July, Two thousand and twelve, make my last will.

To the University Law Library, I leave my collection of rare law volumes and related documents.

To Christopher Collins, I bequeath my autographed edition of Arthur Conan Doyle's The Hound of the Baskervilles, to add to his small but growing collection of rare books.

To Amy Adams, I leave my old rolltop desk. I am sure that she will spend many happy hours discovering its secrets.

To my niece, Christina Ann Jenkins, I leave the family photo album that she may keep it safe and add to it. I also leave her the family silver, the portrait of Thomas Mendez, and my government bonds, worth $5,000, for her school.

The remainder of my estate shall go to my niece, Helene Marie Pleasance, who returned from England to take care of me.

Joseph Manuel Mendez

10-7-12

"There's just got to be something wrong with Mr. Mendez's will," Amy said.

The Secret in the
Stands

They were just minutes away from disaster. Hawkeye knew that if he didn't act quickly, all heck would break loose and the fourth-grade football game would be broken up—and the happy spectators would go running.

Looking around in frustration, Amy nudged Hawkeye. "I don't see anything fishy. Everything seems all right. Maybe it's just a wild goose chase. Are you *sure* some high school seniors are going to try and bust up our game?"

"Yeah," he said, his eyes on the crowd. "Just this morning, John Longbow overheard his big brother talking about it on the phone with another high schooler. He was saying that at half time they were going to pull a great stunt and ruin our game. But I don't see them anywhere."

Amy glanced at the scoreboard clock and let out a nervous sigh. "Yikes! Only five minutes to go until half time. Half our class is out here trying to spot those guys before they can do anything, but it doesn't look like we'll make it."

"We can't just stand here, Amy. You and I have to do something!" said Hawkeye, whipping out his sketch pad and pencil. "Let's be the early birds and catch those worms."

"They sure are worms," muttered Amy. "But I wouldn't want to touch them."

"I remember eating a worm once—when I was a little kid. It didn't taste all that bad, either," Hawkeye said.

"Oh, brother." Amy shook her head and followed him. "Hawkeye, you're genuinely weird sometimes."

Hawkeye grinned. "Thank you," he said graciously.

"Well, let's try to solve this case," Amy said impatiently. "Let's split the stands in half—I'll look at the right half and you check the left."

Hawkeye sat down and decided to sketch his half of the crowd. That way, he might pick up something he'd missed before.

As he sketched, he noticed something odd. When he examined the rest of his sketch, everything fell into place.

Quickly handing the drawing to Amy, he said, "Okay, Amy. The high school seniors who are about to make trouble are right here in my drawing. There are two of them. Let's see if you can find them and figure out what they're about to do. But hurry, or we'll all be sorry!"

"Are you sure some high school seniors are going to try to bust up our game?" asked Amy.

WHERE WERE THE TWO PRANKSTERS AND WHAT WERE THEY ABOUT TO DO?

Find the solution on page 91

The Case of the
Reptile
Rip-Off

Justin was in trouble again. He was always in trouble because he could never turn down a dare. He'd eaten a goldfish from the science lab, hopped like a frog through the police station, and burped into the school intercom system—all because someone had dared him.

So when Justin begged Hawkeye to prove he was innocent of a prank, Hawkeye knew it would be rough, if not impossible, work.

"I swear," said Justin, crossing his heart, "I'm innocent. It's true, a kid in class dared me to sneak into Mrs. McMurtle's house and take her pet boa constrictor. The kid said he'd pay me ten dollars if I was brave enough to do it. Well, I'm brave enough, but I didn't take her stupid snake."

"But Ryan's telling everyone he saw you do it last night," said Hawkeye.

"Ryan's lying. I know him from the football team—he's on the second string—and I've heard him lie before. Hawkeye, you gotta save me. I'm going to get kicked off the football team completely if I get into any more trouble."

"Just be cool." Hawkeye tried to think of some solution. "Don't you have an alibi or something?"

"No. Mom and Dad were out last night. I was home doing my homework." Justin shook his head. "Oh, brother. Mrs. McMurtle's coming home from vacation tomorrow—am I ever going to be in hot water. I swear to you, I didn't steal her snake."

"Come on, let's go see Ryan. If you're really innocent, there has to be some way to prove it."

The two boys hopped on their bikes and rode down Crestview Drive to Ryan's.

"Just let me do the talking," said Hawkeye. "Hey, we better turn on our headlights. It's getting dark fast."

They arrived at Ryan's house a few minutes later. With Justin behind him, Hawkeye knocked on the door. A moment later, Ryan opened it. Hawkeye was frank from the start. "Justin says he didn't steal Mrs.—"

"He's lying," Ryan interrupted. "I looked out the kitchen window and saw someone walking by her house. Then he climbed in the window. It was Justin."

"That's not true!" shouted Justin.

"Shh! I'm doing the talking, remember?" said Hawkeye. "Okay, Ryan, why don't you tell me everything?"

Ryan shrugged. "Well, I was sitting in the kitchen doing my homework. I heard something and looked up. See, I'm supposed to keep an eye on Mrs. McMurtle's house while she's in Florida. I heard a noise and went to the window. It was dark, but I could see someone climbing in the window of her house. After the burglar got in, he turned around and looked out. The moonlight hit him right in the face, and I saw it was Justin."

"Liar!"

"It was you," said Ryan. He turned back to Hawkeye. "Anyway, I ran over to her house to see what was going on. When I got there, the boa constrictor was gone!"

Hawkeye turned to Justin. "You're sure you don't have the snake?"

"Honest, man. You can even come over and search my house."

Ryan glanced to the floor. "Well, maybe he has it hidden in his parents' car or something."

"Don't be ridiculous," snapped Justin.

Hawkeye realized they weren't getting anywhere. But he had a hunch that he wanted to follow up on.

"Ryan," he said, "why don't you show me where you were sitting? I want to make a sketch of what you saw, and then go home and try to figure this out. You know, maybe you made a mistake or something."

"I *didn't* make a mistake." Ryan reluctantly led Hawkeye back to the kitchen.

"Has anyone else been around Mrs. McMurtle's house?" asked Hawkeye.

"I don't know. I don't think so," replied Ryan.

Hawkeye sat down and did a sketch of the view from Ryan's kitchen. He drew for a few minutes, but jumped up before he was quite finished, a big smile on his face.

"That solves that," said Hawkeye, emphatically. "This mystery is a closed case. Justin's innocent."

WHAT DID HAWKEYE SEE THAT PROVED JUSTIN WAS INNOCENT?

Find the solution on page 93

Hawkeye sat down and did a sketch of the view from Ryan's kitchen

The Mystery of the
Musical
Phone Call

"Hawkeye! Sarge just called and said somebody's kidnapped Bobby Banks! That's why he wasn't in school today. Sarge wants us to help find him." Amy spoke urgently into the phone.

"Meet me outside," said Hawkeye. He hung up the phone, shoved his sketch pad and pen into his back pocket, and went outside to wait for Amy.

When she arrived, they raced over to Bobby's house on their bikes. As they rode up, they saw Bobby's mother standing by the pool at the side of the Banks' house, talking to Sergeant Treadwell.

"Hi, Sarge. Hi, Mrs. Banks. I'm sorry about Bobby," said Hawkeye.

"What happened?" asked Amy.

Mrs. Banks was pale and her voice was barely a whisper. "Somebody kidnapped Bobby this morning as he was waiting for the bus to school—right in front of our house! I happened to look out the window and saw Bobby talking to two men in a car. Then I saw one of them pull Bobby into the car, and they drove off."

"Do you know who they were?" Amy asked. "Did you get the license plate number?"

Mrs. Banks shook her head. "No, I was so shaken that I didn't notice anything except that the car was blue."

"Have you gotten a ransom note?" asked Hawkeye.

"No. Sergeant Treadwell is here to install a wire device in case we get any call, but we haven't heard anything yet."

Amy couldn't conceal her dismay. "Don't you have any clues at all?"

"Well," Mrs. Banks said, "when the police asked for help in locating Bobby, Mr. Lefsky, the mailman, told them he had seen Bobby in a blue car turning into Greenwood Cul-de-Sac around eight. Bobby even waved to him. Later, he saw the car come out of the same road, but he didn't notice Bobby inside."

"So we're almost certain that Bobby is in one of the four houses down there, but we don't know which one," Sergeant Treadwell continued. "And we're afraid to search them because we might alarm the kidnappers. First we want to pinpoint which house he's in."

Tears welled up in Mrs. Banks' eyes and she began to sob.

Hawkeye turned to Amy. "Amy, do you want to stay with Mrs. Banks? Maybe the kidnappers will call and you can listen in. I'll be back soon."

On his bike, Hawkeye headed for Greenwood Cul-de-Sac. The four houses were at the end of the wooded road by the lake. Hawkeye stopped before he reached the houses, hid his bike in the bushes, and crept forward to a spot in the underbrush where he could see the houses without being seen. Then he carefully examined each house, looking for clues.

But he was disappointed. All was still— it seemed that the kidnappers were being careful. Feeling his stomach rumble, Hawkeye realized he was probably already late for dinner. He pulled out his pad and quickly sketched the four houses.

"I'll just check with Amy to see if the kidnappers called," he thought, "and then I'll head home. I'd better not be too late—even if this is an important case."

As he approached Bobby's house, he saw Amy sitting on the front steps. She leaped to her feet. "Hawkeye, Bobby's just called—the kidnappers want Mr. Banks to meet one of them tonight with a hundred thousand dollars!"

Hawkeye gasped. "Boy, what a lot of money! Did you get any clues? What else did Bobby say?"

Amy was so excited that she grabbed Hawkeye by the hand and pulled him into the house. "Listen for yourself," she said. "Sarge recorded it. Bobby's voice is shaky and there's a lot of funny beeping, but you can still hear him. He says some weird things—I think he was trying to give us some clues."

Hawkeye turned on the recording and heard Bobby's voice. "Hi, Mom, it's me—Bobby. Mom... *Beep! Beep! Beep!*... Mom, I'm okay but I'm so cold. They won't light the fire. And they say that they're going to lock me in a room upstairs and starve me if Dad doesn't meet them tonight at Mill Creek Bridge and give them a hundred thousand dollars... *Beep! Beep! Beep!*"

There was a slight pause, and then a snarling voice said, "That's enough outta you, kid!" Then the phone was slammed down and the line went dead. Hawkeye stopped the machine.

"Bobby's smart," he said. "I think you're right. He's got to be trying to tell us something. Those beeps—what would cause them?"

Amy walked over to the Banks' phone and picked up the receiver. Thoughtfully, she pushed a few buttons. Suddenly, she wheeled around to face Hawkeye.

"That's it—those beeps! Bobby was pushing the buttons on the phone as he talked. Let's play the tape again."

Excitedly, she rewound the tape and they listened as it played.

"That's 'Three Blind Mice'! Bobby was playing 'Three Blind Mice' on his phone!" Amy yelled.

"What could that mean?" asked Hawkeye. "Hmm. Let's look at the houses." He pulled out his sketch pad and he and Amy looked at the drawings of the four houses.

"Got it! I know which house it is. Hey, Sarge!" shouted Hawkeye.

"Bobby is in one of the four houses, but we don't know which one," Sergeant Treadwell concluded.

WHICH HOUSE WAS BOBBY IN, AND HOW DID HAWKEYE KNOW?

Find the solution on page 95

The Secret of the Smuggler's Car

Sergeant Treadwell was in disguise again. He had on a wig of bluish-grey hair, a red polka-dot dress, and nice white leather shoes. He sat on a park bench, trying to smile like a sweet little old lady.

Hawkeye, wearing a black wig and a big hat, sat on one side of him. Amy, wearing fake glasses, sat on the other.

"This is a good reason not to be a cop," said Hawkeye, laughing. "You sure must love your work to dress up like that."

"Shh," whispered Sergeant Treadwell as he straightened his wig. In a high voice, he added, "You two are supposed to be my grandchildren—so for heaven's sake, be kind to me! Besides, what could be more innocent than a little old lady?"

"No offense, Sarge," said Amy, "but most little old ladies look a lot smaller and older than you. You'd be more convincing if you didn't have such big shoulders and such a baby face."

"Shh," he whispered again. "Here comes Sly Malone's car."

They were sitting in Von Buttermore Park, across the street from Sam's Service Station. For a couple of weeks now, Sergeant Treadwell had suspected that Sly Malone, a known criminal, was smuggling stolen platinum from the U.S. into Canada. Each time Sly crossed the border, customs officials searched his car, but so far they hadn't found a single sign of the "white gold."

"The only thing I know," continued Sergeant Treadwell in his little old lady voice, "is that every afternoon for the past three days he's come to this garage. Now, what could be so special about Sam's Service Station?"

"Maybe he's having a lot of trouble with his car," suggested Amy.

"Or else something fishy is going on inside the garage," said Hawkeye.

Sergeant Treadwell nodded. "Yeah, but I haven't noticed anything. Let's just wait and see what happens. There's his car. Hawkeye, you have your pad and pencil. See if you can come up with anything."

"Hurry," whispered Amy. "The car is pulling up to the garage."

Hawkeye whipped out his pad and pencil and started to draw as fast as he could.

Sly Malone, his hair greased down, pulled his big red sedan up to the garage door. He got out and went into the office. A moment later, a mechanic came out and climbed into the car.

Amy clenched her fists. "Hurry!" she hissed.

The large garage door opened and the mechanic drove in. Hawkeye completed his sketch before the door closed again.

"That's exactly what happened yesterday and the day before," said Sergeant Treadwell. "Sly got out, a mechanic pulled the car in, and an hour later, Sly drove the car out. If only I knew what was going on inside!"

Hawkeye, Amy, and Sergeant Treadwell sat on the park bench for more than an hour, waiting for Sly to leave. While they waited, an old man came up and stood directly in front of Sergeant Treadwell. The old man smiled and nodded at the trio on the bench.

"Nice day, isn't it?" said the old man.

The sergeant wasn't sure what to do. After a moment of desperation, he replied in his high voice, "Ahem, I... I suppose it is."

"Nice day to go out to dinner. Care to join me for a bite to eat? Your grandchildren, too, of course."

Sergeant Treadwell stood up, adjusting his dress and teetering back and forth on his high heels. He looked down at the man. "No thanks, buddy!"

The old man appeared to be more surprised by the sergeant's size than anything else.

"Oh, perhaps another time, then!" he exclaimed, hurrying away.

Hawkeye and Amy broke into laughter when the man was out of earshot.

"When he saw that you were about twice as big as he was, I think he was happy you turned him down, Sarge," said Amy, chuckling.

A few minutes later, Sly Malone backed his car out of the garage. Sergeant Treadwell glanced at the car and threw up his hands.

"Nothing! Nothing again. I'm sure he's smuggling platinum into Canada, but I can't figure out how."

"Wait a minute," said Amy. "Hawkeye, quick. Sketch the car again."

"You bet. I think I see what you mean."

Hawkeye tore off the first sketch and started again. As Sly backed out, Hawkeye quickly drew the car. He and Amy noticed a number of details. By the time Hawkeye had finished his second sketch, they'd solved the case.

"Here you go, Sarge." Hawkeye proudly handed him the two drawings.

Amy said, "Just take a close look at these and you'll see how Sly Malone is smuggling the platinum across the border!"

"Sly got out, a mechanic pulled the car in,
and an hour later, Sly drove the car out," said Sarge.

HOW WAS SLY MALONE SMUGGLING THE PLATINUM?

Find the solution on page 97

The Secret of the
Ancient
Treasure

Part 4
The Treasure Trove

What Happened in Volumes 1, 2, and 3
When Hawkeye and Amy were looking for fossils in
a cave along Mill Creek, they discovered an old metal
box buried deep in one of the underground rooms.
Inside the box was a yellowed, frayed map, which
clearly led to the von Buttermore estate. On the map
were some letters and numbers written in code. Amy
broke the code, which led them to the old stable on
the von Buttermore estate.

Mrs. von Buttermore guessed that the map was connected with the theft, eighty years ago, of her grandfather's priceless collection of ancient Egyptian gems and statuettes. As Hawkeye, Amy, and Mrs. von Buttermore were searching the stable for a clue that would lead them to the treasure, Amy fell through a trap door into a secret room. There, they found some of the Egyptian treasure and a rebus—a picture code—that they hoped would lead them to the rest of the treasure.

At the end of "The Mysterious Message" (Part 3 of "The Secret of the Ancient Treasure"), Amy had just cracked the picture code.

"Maybe the rebus will tell us where the Egyptian treasures are hidden!" exclaimed Hawkeye.

The Treasure Trove

"The rebus has something to do with tennis and something to do with bugs," Amy explained to Hawkeye and Mrs. von Buttermore. "See, this is someone serving, and these are ants."

"Serve... ants... no." Mrs. von Buttermore pondered this for a moment, then suddenly understood. "Oh, I see. 'Servants know'!"

"And the next part is, 'I have treasure,'" said Hawkeye, excitedly pointing to the pictures. "'Servants know I have the Egyptian treasure.'"

"And then come the directions." Amy took a breath. "'Go... through... tunnel... upstairs... to... drawing... room.'"

"Drawing room?" gasped Mrs. von Buttermore. "My drawing room? You don't suppose anything could be there, do you?"

"I don't know," said Hawkeye. "But I sure want to find out."

Amy aimed the flashlight down the passageway. "And the rebus says we're supposed to go through the tunnel."

Mrs. von Buttermore strode toward the passageway. "Why, I haven't had so much fun since I went sledding in the Yukon last year!"

Guided by the beam of the flashlight, the three of them started down the passage leading out of the secret room. Only a few feet wide, the tunnel went straight for a while and then started twisting back and forth.

Glancing up, Hawkeye noticed that the ceiling was supported by wooden boards. He looked down. "Hey, the floors are just dirt," he said. "I wonder where this tunnel goes."

A little impatiently, Amy said, "The rebus said to go through the tunnel, so let's just go."

Several minutes later, they came to a door at the end of the passage. Amy opened the bolt, but the hinge was so rusted that she couldn't push the door open.

"Rats," she said.

Hawkeye stepped forward and began pounding on the door.

"Hey, wait a minute. Listen." Amy cupped her ear against the door. "It sounds like there's a machine in there!"

"Heavens, where are we?" said Mrs. von Buttermore, adjusting her sari. "This tunnel's made so many turns that I haven't the faintest idea where we are. We could be near the house, or even the lake."

Hawkeye said, "Well, the rebus said to take the tunnel to the stairs to the drawing room, so I'd guess we're near your house."

He pounded on the corners of the door. Suddenly, they heard a scream from the other side of the door.

Hawkeye hissed over his shoulder, "Someone's in trouble! I can't get the door open!"

Amy joined him in pounding on the door, but it still wouldn't budge.

"Come on!" Mrs. von Buttermore took a few steps backward and bent over slightly. "If we all run straight at that door, I bet we can break it open."

The screams on the other side of the door became louder and louder. Something awful was happening.

"Right," said Amy.

Hawkeye and Amy took up ramming positions next to Mrs. von Buttermore. They bent over, stuck out their shoulders, and prepared to charge forward.

"Ready?" asked Hawkeye. "Good. One, two, three, go!"

The trio raced forward and bashed straight into the old, wooden door. Under the force, the door shivered and finally broke away from its hinges. They came crashing through the door in a shower of plaster, and fell on top of one another. The person screaming was out of control, her hands clenched, her mouth wide open.

Mrs. von Buttermore picked herself up. "My word, we're in the basement of my house!" She turned to the woman who had been screaming, but who was now standing transfixed.

"Emma, dear!" Mrs. von Buttermore brushed herself off and went over to the younger woman. "It's all right. I'm sorry we scared you so."

Hawkeye and Amy got up and dusted themselves off, too.

"Wow," said Hawkeye, "the secret passage had been plastered over."

"Yeah, it must've been an escape passage." Amy picked up one of the boards.

"I've only been down here a few times," said Mrs. von Buttermore, "but I'm certain you couldn't tell from the inside that there was a door here." She turned back to the maid and patted her on the shoulder.

"It's all right, Emma. It's only us."

Emma, brushing away a few tears, continued to shake.

"Oh, Mrs. von Buttermore, I was down here loading the dryer and... and I heard this pounding behind one of the walls. And then... then... the three of you just exploded out of a blank wall! I was so scared!"

Amy nodded in sympathy. "Well, I would've been, too."

After Emma was calmer, Hawkeye, Amy, and Mrs. von Buttermore looked at each other. Almost in chorus, they said, "The drawing room!"

They charged up the back stairs, startling more servants as they tore through the kitchen.

"To think that all this time Grandpapa's collection might have been right in my very own drawing room!" Mrs. von Buttermore exclaimed.

Amy slid around a corner. "And how many times have Hawkeye and I been there?"

"Yeah, maybe we've been looking right at them," said Hawkeye.

Panting, they entered the drawing room. They stood motionless and gazed around them. But the high-ceilinged room appeared just as it always did—elegant, but not in the least mysterious. There were several large windows (overlooking a rose garden), a fireplace, some comfortable chairs, a couch, a writing desk, and Priceless, Mrs. von Buttermore's black and white Great Dane, still asleep in the sun.

Brushing some plaster from her hair, Mrs. von Buttermore said, "Heavens, I don't see anything unusual. The room looks like it always has. Perhaps Dr. T got away with Grandpapa's Egyptian collection, after all."

Disappointed, she sank into a chair. Amy went to her side.

"We can't give up yet, Mrs. von Buttermore," she said. "We've got to follow through with it all—that's what all good sleuths do—and find the answer, whether it's yes or no."

Hawkeye paced around the room. His eyes roved everywhere, checking out the corners, the ceiling, the walls, and the furniture.

"That's right," he said. He hit on an idea. "Hey, maybe they changed this room. You know, it might be different now from the way it was back then. That'd be why we can't see the clue. Mrs. von Buttermore, didn't you say the room was being remodeled at the time of the robbery?"

Mrs. von Buttermore sat up and put her hand to her mouth. "Oh, my dear, you're right." She stood up, her sari brushing the floor, and began to walk about. "Now, let me see..." While Mrs. von Buttermore strained to remember everything she could and Amy searched the room, Hawkeye pulled out his sketch pad and pencil. He sat down in a large, soft chair and studied the room. Stroking his chin, he noted all the important details before he began to draw.

Hawkeye took his time with the drawing. If the Egyptian treasures really were in the room, they could be hidden anywhere—in the walls, in the floor, even in the furniture.

"Boy," he said to himself, "if Dr. T hid them in the furniture, we're in trouble. I bet a lot of things have changed since the robbery."

Mrs. von Buttermore tapped her chin with her finger. "Let's see."

She went to a cabinet beneath the built-in bookshelves, and opened one pair of doors, then another. Then she hastily began to go through a pile of things.

"I thought so!" she said, pulling a large photo album from the cabinet. "There's a picture in here of this room that was taken before the remodeling and the robbery."

She laid the album on the table and thumbed through it. Hawkeye and Amy hurried to her side.

"Here it is!" said Mrs. von Buttermore.

The old, brown photograph she held in her hand obviously had been taken many, many years ago.

"Hawkeye," said Amy, "put your sketch next to the photo and let's compare them."

He placed the drawing right alongside the photograph. All three of them scanned the sketch and the picture, searching for similarities and differences.

"There's something different about the way the room looks," Hawkeye said slowly. Although the room did not appear to be changed much, he sensed that some portion of it had been altered very subtly.

Finally, Hawkeye snapped his fingers and broke the silence. "I got it! I know where the Egyptian treasure is hidden!"

WHERE WAS THE EGYPTIAN TREASURE TROVE HIDDEN?

Find the solution on page 99

The Egyptian treasures could be hidden anywhere;
in the walls, in the floor, even in the furniture.

Solution

The Case of the
Imperfect Crime

Hawkeye noticed a number of things that told him who had stolen the painting. First, the fact that the wallet, the silverware, and the other painting had not been stolen seemed peculiar.

"I don't understand why the thief didn't take as much as possible," he said. It also seemed strange to him that the scissors, which apparently had been used to cut the phone cord, had been put away so neatly. Finally, Hawkeye noticed that the glass on the door was broken outward, not inward. If someone had broken into the house from the patio, the glass would have landed in the living room. And only one person would have been likely to break the glass from inside the house.

"Mrs. Peterson!" exclaimed Hawkeye.

When confronted, Mrs. Peterson confessed that she had faked the burglary to get the insurance money. Sergeant Treadwell gave her a stern lecture and helped her re-hang the painting.

Solution

The Case of the
Mysterious Dognapper

Although a number of people had a motive for dog-napping Priceless, it was the butler who did it. The clue that tipped off Hawkeye and Amy was that it was the Fourth of July, and there isn't any mail delivery on that day—it's a national holiday. Ives had written the letter himself and put it in Mrs. von Buttermore's mailbox, but he had forgotten that it should be postmarked.

"And look at this letter," said Amy. "Only an Englishman would have written 'CENTRE,' and 'RING UP.' That proves that Ives is the dognapper".

Ives begged for mercy, saying he did it only because he was allergic to Priceless and needed the money to get away. Mrs. von Buttermore fired him, but gave him two weeks' pay to help him in his job hunt.

When she got Priceless back, Mrs. von Buttermore was so happy that she not only donated the youth center to the city, but threw in a swimming pool, too.

Solution

The Mystery of the
Moody Medallion

From Hawkeye's sketch, Amy noticed that there was something else behind Mr. Moody's back in the painting itself: a clock, sitting on the fireplace mantel. The riddle had said that "one face alone" would provide a clue, and Amy realized that the clock, too, had a face.

Hawkeye jumped up and ran over to the fireplace. He reached up and took the clock in his hands.

"Amy, you're right!," he said, examining the circular weight at the end of the pendulum. "The medallion's right here!"

Because Amy had been the one to figure out Mr. Moody's riddle, Hawkeye tried to give her the medallion. But she wouldn't take it. A month later, the nephew took over the Moody mansion. When he heard about how Hawkeye and Amy had found the medallion, he decided to give Amy the clock it had been hidden in.

Solution

The Case of the
Stashed Cash

Amy suddenly realized that "Knight to K2" was a code for a chess move. "It tells a player to move his knight to the square right in front of the one where his king starts the game!" she cried.

Mr. Bertolini got a crowbar and pried up the tile Amy pointed to on the floor.

Frank had indeed hidden the money under the tile. The tile lay one row out from the base of the counter, directly in front of the cardboard circle that showed the size of the king-size pizza. That tile would be called "K2" in chess-player's code.

Mr. Bertolini was delighted. "This is wonderful, fantastic! Hawkeye, Amy, how can I thank you?"

They looked at one another and grinned.

"How about a king-size pizza—with everything on it?" said Hawkeye.

"Yeah," agreed Amy. "But no pepperoni on my half."

Solution

The Mystery of the
Double-Crossed Inheritance

Hawkeye spotted something that seemed to indicate that the will had been forged.

In his last reading of the will, he saw that the date written at the top was different from the date beside the signature. The month and day beside the signature were reversed. July is not the tenth month, but the seventh.

"And look at this, Dad," he said, pleading their case. "The sevens are crossed. Americans don't write the date with the day first, and they don't cross their sevens. But someone from England might."

"And, Mr. Collins," added Amy, "who had the skill to forge the will? Miss Pleasance. You know, because of all the penmanship stuff she does for the greeting card company."

The next day, Mr. Collins had the will examined and found that it had indeed been forged. The real will, which Sergeant Treadwill later found in Miss Pleasance's desk, left the majority of the estate to Christina. Hawkeye and Amy got to keep the book and desk they had inherited from Mr. Mendez, but they also got a stern warning from Mr. Collins.

"Next time you have a question like that," he said, shaking a finger at them, "you come and see me before you go snooping around."

Solution

The Secret in the
Stands

Hawkeye had noticed a nurse in uniform standing by the trainer's shed. But when he started to draw her, he saw that "she" had a faint beard and mustache. He realized that the "nurse" was one of the guys from the high school. Then he spotted a policeman in a uniform that obviously didn't fit.

Hawkeye then noticed that the "nurse" was standing near a garden-hose faucet on the side of the shed. He traced the hose through the crowd and up to the top of the bleachers, where the fake policeman stood, holding the nozzle of the hose.

Amy looked for a long moment at the drawing that showed all this. "All right, all right," she finally yelled. "I see them. Now let's top them before they spray everyone!"

Hawkeye and Amy dashed to the top of the bleachers, grabbed the hose, and pointed it at the high schooler who was disguised as a nurse. When the referee blew the whistle for half time, the "nurse" turned on the water—and got soaked!

Solution

The Case of the
Reptile Rip-Off

Hawkeye saw the position of the moon rising over Mrs. McMurtle's house.

"There's no way Ryan could have seen Justin the way he said he did," said Hawkeye. "The moon is right behind Mrs. McMurtle's house. Therefore, the moonlight couldn't have hit Justin in the face."

In the end, Ryan admitted that he had stolen Mrs. McMurtle's boa constrictor. "It's down in the basement," he said, squirming with embarrassment. "Oh, no! Mom's starting to do the laundry!" Ryan put his hand over his mouth. "The washing machine was empty and I hid the snake in there!"

Ryan later told Hawkeye that he had wanted Justin's spot on the football team and he thought he might get it if Justin were kicked off the team. Instead, by order of his mother, Ryan was suspended from playing for a month.

After being found in the bathtub, the snake was returned to Mrs. McMurtle.

Solution

The Mystery of the
Musical Phone Call

Hawkeye knew from Bobby's phone call that the house he was being kept in had two stories, because he had said that his kidnappers had threatened to lock him "in a room upstairs."

Hawkeye also knew the house had to have a chimney because Bobby had said the kidnappers wouldn't light the fire. The song "Three Blind Mice" could only describe the two houses that have three windows.

From these clues, Hawkeye figured out that Bobby was being kept in the house in the upper-right-hand corner of his sketch. He explained his reasoning to Sergeant Treadwell, who reached Bobby just after the kidnappers had left to collect the ransom money.

Bobby was unharmed, the kidnappers were captured, and the money was recovered. Mr. and Mrs. Banks gave Hawkeye and Amy each a crisp, fifty-dollar bill. And so everything turned out well—except that Hawkeye itched for three days from the poison ivy he had touched while he crouched in the bushes.

Solution

The Secret of the
Smuggler's Car

Sly Malone was smuggling platinum by carefully hiding it on the car.

"Look how different the car was after Sly left the garage," said Hawkeye.

Amy pointed to the drawing. "You see? There are new hubcaps, new bumpers, and a wider metal strip on the side. And, look, there's an antennae and a side mirror now, too. I bet you all that stuff isn't chrome—it's platinum!"

Sergeant Treadwell kicked off shoes, tore off his wig, ran to his squad car, and radioed an alert to the station. The police caught Sly and found the platinum. Sly was sent to prison for five years.

Solution

The Secret of the
Ancient Treasure

The Egyptian treasure was hidden in two secret compartments in Mrs. von Buttermore's drawing room. In comparing the photograph and the drawing, Hawkeye noticed something different about the way the light was entering the room. Carefully examining the windows, he realized that they were now smaller than they used to be.

"That created a space underneath each window for a secret compartment," said Hawkeye.

"Wow, you're right!" said Amy. She ran over to the area beneath one of the windows and knocked on the wood. "It sounds hollow!"

Mrs. von Buttermore ordered a crowbar. When the butler returned with one on a silver platter, she snatched it and quickly began to pry at the edge of the windowsills. A board came loose, and Hawkeye and Amy pulled it free. There, below the window, was part of the collection of Egyptian treasures, carefully hidden eighty years ago.

So for eighty years, the Egyptian treasures had remained hidden away.

Later, they reconstructed what had happened: when Grandpapa von Buttermore had hurt himself during the remodeling of the room, Dr. T had ordered him to stay in bed for three weeks. Either during this time or before Grandpapa's accident, Dr. T had copied the keys to the library and had begun stealing the Egyptian artifacts. One by one, he had hidden them in the drawing room. He had planned to put them all in the secret room beneath the stable, but the servants had become suspicious of his trips to the basement.

Dr. T had then hired the professional thief, Jesse Carter, to get the items out of the mansion. At about that time, though, Dr. T's plot was discovered and he was run out of town. And before he could get the artifacts, Jesse Carter was arrested and jailed for a previous bank robbery.

Mrs. von Buttermore donated almost all of the artifacts to the Lakewood Hills Museum. There was a long article in the newspaper, and Hawkeye and Amy got their pictures on the front page.

Best of all, Mrs. von Buttermore gave Hawkeye the statuette of Horus, the hawk-headed Egyptian god. And she gave Amy a beautiful gold Egyptian necklace with an amulet on it that kept away evil eyes.

The Girls to the Rescue Series

Edited by Bruce Lansky

Here are seven collections of stories featuring heroic, clever, and determined girls from around the world. Each book contains tales about girls such as Emily, who helps a runaway slave and her baby reach safety and freedom, and Kamala, a Punjabi girl who outsmarts a pack of thieves. This series for girls ages 7 to 13 has received critical acclaim and raves from mothers and daughters alike.

Can You Solve the Mystery Series

Twelve-year-old amateur sleuths and best friends Hawkeye Collins and Amy Adams love to solve cases. They invite readers to follow clues and sketches to solve crimes in their hometown of Lakewood Hills. All of the books in the Can You Solve the Mystery? series contain 9-10 short mysteries. Readers are given written and visual clues to help them solve the crime. The answers and a brief wrap-up are given in the back of the book. This series is for curious children ages 6 to 13.

⚏ Meadowbrook Press

6110 Blue Circle Drive, Suite 237, Minnetonka, MN 55343

www.MeadowbrookPress.com